GALLANT OLD ENGINE

by

The Rev. W. Awdry

with illustrations by
John T. Kenney

GROLIER

Passengers and Polish

NANCY is a Guard's daughter. She was working on Skarloey with some polish and a rag.

"Wake up lazy-bones!" she said severely. "Your brass is filthy. Aren't you ashamed?"

"No," said Skarloey sleepily. "You're just an old fusspot. Go away!"

She tickled his nose. "Rheneas comes home tomorrow. Don't you want to look nice?"

Skarloey woke suddenly. "What! Tomorrow!"

"Yes, Daddy told me. I'm going now."

"Nancy, Stop! Do I look really nice? Please polish me again. There's a good kind girl."

"Now who's an old fusspot?" laughed Nancy.

She gave him another rub, then climbed down.

"Aren't you going to polish me?" asked Duncan.

"Sorry, not today. I'm helping the Refreshment Lady this afternoon. We must get the ices and things ready for the Passengers on Skarloey's two o'clock train. Never mind, Duncan, I'll give you a good polish tomorrow."

But Duncan did mind. "It isn't fair!" he complained. "Peter Sam gets a special funnel, Sir Handel special wheels, Passengers get ices, and I'm never even polished."

This, of course, wasn't true; but Duncan liked having a grievance. He began to sulk.

That afternoon a message came from the Station by the Waterfall. "One of Skarloey's coaches has come off the rails. Please send some workmen to put it right."

Duncan was "in steam", so he had to go.

"All this extra work," he grumbled, "it wears an engine out!"

"Rubbish," said his Driver. "Come on!"

The derailed coach was in the middle of his train, so Skarloey had gone on to the Top Station with the front coaches. Duncan left the workmen, and brought the Passengers in the rear coaches home. He sulked all the way.

He arrived back just in time for his own four o'clock train. "I get no rest! I get no rest!" he complained.

He was sulky and short of steam, so his Driver waited a few minutes in the hope of raising more; but Duncan wouldn't try.

"We can't keep the Passengers waiting any longer," his Driver said at last.

"You always think about Passengers," muttered Duncan crossly, "and never about *me*. I'm never even polished. I'm overworked, and I won't stand it."

He grumbled away, brooding over his "wrongs".

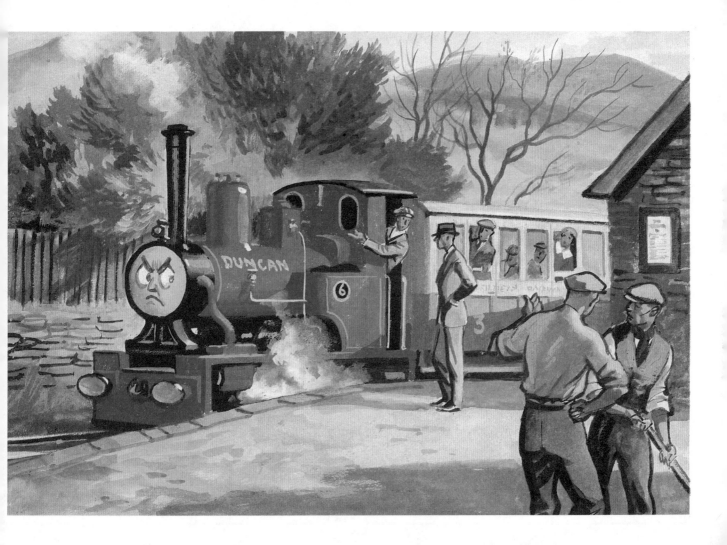

Duncan made "heavy weather" of the journey, but at last they reached the Viaduct. This is long, high and narrow. No one can walk on it when a train is there.

"Come on, Duncan!" said his Driver. "One more effort, and you'll have a rest and a drink in the Station."

"Keep your old Station!" said Duncan rudely. "I'm staying here!"

He did too! He stopped his train right on the Viaduct, and nothing his Driver or Fireman could do would make him move another yard.

Skarloey came from the Top Station to haul Duncan and his train to the platform. The Passengers were very cross. They burst out of the train, and told the Drivers, the Firemen, and the Guard what a Bad Railway it was.

Skarloey had to pull the train to the Top Station, too. Duncan wouldn't even try.

The Thin Controller was waiting at the Shed for Duncan that evening. He spoke to him severely. But Duncan still stayed sulky. He muttered to himself, "No polish, no Passengers," in an obstinate sort of voice.

Gallant Old Engine

"I'm ashamed of you, Duncan," said Skarloey. "You should think of your Passengers."

"Passengers are just nuisances. They're always complaining."

Skarloey was shocked. "That's no way to talk," he said. "Passengers are our coal and water. No Passengers means no trains. No trains means no Railway. Then we'd be on the scrap-heap, my engine, and don't you forget it. Thank goodness Rheneas is coming home. Perhaps he'll teach you sense before it's too late."

"What has Rheneas to do with it?"

"Rheneas saved our Railway," said Skarloey.

"Please tell us about it," begged Peter Sam.

"The year before you came," said the old engine, "things were very bad. We were on our last wheels. Mr Hugh was Driver and Fireman, while the Thin Controller was Guard. He did everything else too, *and* helped Mr Hugh mend us in the Shed.

" 'We expect two fresh engines next year,' they told us, 'but we *must* keep the trains going *now*; if we don't, our Railway will close.' "

"How awful!" said Peter Sam in sympathy.

"I tried hard, though I couldn't do much, but Rheneas understood. 'It's my turn now,' he said. 'You've done more than your share of hard work.' "

He was often short of steam, but he always tried to struggle to a Station, and rest there. "That," said Skarloey earnestly, "is *most* important with Passengers."

"Pshaw!" exclaimed Duncan.

"Passengers," Skarloey continued, "don't mind stopping at Stations. They can get out and walk about. That's what Stations are for. But they get very cross if we stop at wrong places like Viaducts. Then they say we're a Bad Railway, and never come back.

"I remember Rheneas stopping in a wrong place once," said Skarloey. "He couldn't help it. But he made up for it afterwards.

"That afternoon he had damp rails and a full train. There were Passengers even in Beatrice, the Guard's van. His wheels slipped dreadfully on the steep bit after the first Station, but they gripped at last. 'The worst's over,' he thought. 'Now we're away.'

" 'Come along, come along,' he sang to the coaches. 'Come al—— Oooooh! I've got Cramp!' he groaned. He stopped, unable to move, on the loneliest part of the line.

"The Thin Controller and Mr Hugh examined him carefully. The Passengers watched and waited. Rheneas eyed them anxiously. They looked cross.

"At last the Thin Controller stood up. 'Your valve gear on one side had jammed,' he said. 'We've unfastened the rods and tied them up. Now Rheneas,' he went on, 'we need to reach the next Station. Can you pull us there on one cylinder?'

" 'I'll try, Sir, but the next Station isn't the right Station. Will the Passengers be cross?'

" 'Don't worry,' smiled the Thin Controller. 'They know we can't reach the Top Station today.'

"The Thin Controller sanded the rails, Passengers from Beatrice pushed behind; Mr Hugh gently eased out the regulator. The train jerked and began to move.

" 'I'll . . . do . . . . it! I'll . . . do . . . . it!'

"Everyone cheered, but Rheneas heard nothing. 'The Thin Controller's relying on me. If I fail, the Railway will close. It mustn't! It mustn't! I'll get there or burst.'

"Everything blurred. He was too tired to move another yard; but he did! And another . . . and another . . . and another . . . till, 'I've got there at last,' he sighed with relief.

" 'It's proud of you I am indeed,' said Mr Hugh.

"All Rheneas remembered about the journey down was having to go on going on. At the Big Station the Passengers thanked him.

" 'We expected a long walk,' they said, 'but you brought us home. We'll come again, and bring our friends.'

" 'You're a gallant little engine,' said the Thin Controller. 'When you're rested, we'll mend you ready for tomorrow.' "

"Was Rheneas always 'ready for tomorrow'?"

"Always," smiled Skarloey. "Whatever happened, Rheneas always pulled his trains."

It was Duncan who broke the silence. "Thank you for telling us about Rheneas," he said. "I was wrong. Passengers *are* important after all."

All the Little Engines were at the Wharf on the day that Rheneas came home.

Some of the Fat Controller's Engines were there too.

Edward pushed Rheneas' truck to the siding, and Skarloey pulled him neatly to his own rails. This was the signal for a chorus of whistles from engines large and small. You never heard such a noise in all your life!

The Owner, Rheneas, and other Important People made speeches, the Band played and everyone was very happy.

But Rheneas was happiest of all in his own place that night, next to his friend Skarloey. "This helps a little engine to feel," he said, "that, at last, he has really come home."

This book club edition published by Grolier 1995

Published by arrangement with Reed Children's Books
First published in Great Britain 1962 as part of *The Railway Series* No. 17
Copyright © William Heinemann Ltd. 1962
This edition copyright © William Heinemann Ltd. 1995